MARINA LIBRARY

JUL 1 0 1998

P9-BYZ-223

EEK!
Stories to make you shriek™

For Beginning Readers
Ages 6-8

This series of spooky stories has been created especially for beginning readers—children in first and second grades who are developing their reading skills.

How do these books help children learn to read?

- Kids love creepy stories and these stories are true page-turners (but never too scary).
- The sentences are short.
- The words are simple and repeated often in the story.
- The type is large with lots of room between words and lines.
- Full-color pictures on every page act as visual "clues" to help children figure out the words on the page.

Once children have read one story, they'll be asking for more!

For my sister, Laura Pfeifer—J.D.

To my daughter Anna, my first editor—S.L.

Text copyright © 1996 by Jennifer Dussling. Illustrations copyright © 1996 by Sonja Lamut. All rights reserved. Published by Grosset & Dunlap, Inc., which is a member of The Putnam & Grosset Group, New York. EEK! STORIES TO MAKE YOU SHRIEK is a trademark of The Putnam & Grosset Group. GROSSET & DUNLAP is a trademark of Grosset & Dunlap, Inc. Published simultaneously in Canada. Printed in the U.S.A.

Library of Congress Cataloging-in-Publication Data

Dussling, Jennifer.
    A very strange dollhouse / by Jennifer Dussling ; illustrated by
Sonja Lamut.
        p.   cm. — (Eek! Stories to make you shriek)
    Summary: Lucy, the new girl at school, invites a classmate to play
with her unusual dollhouse..
    [1. Dollhouses—Fiction.   2. Horror stories.]   I. Lamut, Sonja, ill.
II. Title.   III. Series.
PZ7.D943Ve   1996
[Fic]—dc20   95-46793
                                                                                         CIP
                                                                                         AC
ISBN 0-448-41346-9 (GB)   A B C D E F G H I J
ISBN 0-448-41311-6 (pb)   A B C D E F G H I J

Easy-to-Read
Ages 6–8

EEK!

Stories to make you shriek™

A Very Strange Dollhouse

By Jennifer Dussling

Illustrated by Sonja Lamut

Public Library San Mateo, CA

Grosset & Dunlap • New York

Lucy was new in school.

Right away, nobody liked her.

"She is weird,"

said my friend Ann.

But Lucy liked me.

She told me so the first day.

She followed me everywhere—

to lunch,

to gym,

to the bathroom.

"Can I come to your house?"

she asked me. "Please !"

"I guess . . ." I said.

Lucy <u>was</u> a little weird.

But I wanted to be nice.

The next day after school,

Lucy came over.

"Do you want to play jacks?"

I asked her.

"Or cards, or . . ."

Lucy was not listening to me.

She was walking across my room.

There was a strange look on her face.

"Oh, what pretty dolls!" she said.

Lucy picked one up.

"I always wanted a doll

with dark eyes and brown hair."

Then she stared at me.

"Just like you!" she said quietly.

I did not like

the creepy look on Lucy's face.

So I said quickly,

"Want to see my best doll?"

I got out an old doll trunk.

"This doll belonged

to my great-grandmother,"

I told Lucy.

Then I started to brag a little.

"This doll is almost

a hundred years old.

She is worth loads of money."

Lucy looked at me funny.

She ran her hand slowly

across the doll's dress.

"That's nothing," she said.

"I have a dollhouse.

And the little dolls in it

are one of a kind."

I shook my head.

"Nobody has

one-of-a-kind dolls!"

I said.

"But they are," Lucy said.

"You will see."

When Lucy said that,

I got a creepy feeling

on the back of my neck.

"And you will be sorry

that you did not believe me,"

she said.

Lucy shoved the doll at me

and walked out of my room.

I figured that was the end of Lucy.

And I did not care.

She <u>was</u> weird.

But the next morning at school,

Lucy ran right up to me.

She was not mad at all.

She was all sweet and nice.

"I forgot to thank you

for having me over,"

Lucy said.

"Come to my house today.

I will let you play

with my dollhouse."

Lucy's eyes got a funny look.

"My very special dollhouse."

I still thought Lucy was pretty strange.

But I really wanted to see this dollhouse.

And her one-of-a-kind dolls.

So I went to her house after school.

Lucy's house was pretty.

It was white,

with green shutters and pink curtains.

Everything was very neat inside.

It was very quiet, too.

It made me a little nervous.

"Are your parents home?" I asked.

"They are around.

You will meet them later,"

was all she said.

Lucy took me to her room.

In one corner was a great big dollhouse.

I forgot about Lucy acting weird.

I forgot about the super-neat house.

All I could think about

was this amazing dollhouse.

It was white with green shutters.

And there were pink curtains

in the windows.

It was just like Lucy's house!

Lucy turned the dollhouse around.

Lots of stuff inside looked the same, too!

The sofa looked like

the sofa in the real living room.

24

Two dolls were by the sofa.

A mother and a father.

"These dolls look so real—
like little people," I said.

Lucy sighed.

"I wish I had more," she said.

"I wish I had kid dolls too.

I am going to get one very soon."

She smiled.

All of a sudden

I got that creepy feeling

on my neck again.

I turned back to the dollhouse.

I looked at

the mother and father dolls.

They were by the window.

Something seemed wrong.

Then it hit me.

Weren't they by the sofa just a second ago?

But how did they move?

I had to be wrong.

I looked closely at the dolls.

Their faces looked worried. . . .

No . . . that was not quite it.

They looked scared.

I started to pick one up.

But Lucy grabbed my hand.

"I am so glad you came over,"

Lucy told me.

"You are such a good friend.

Come back tomorrow.

You can play in the dollhouse then."

I frowned at Lucy.

"Don't you mean

with the dollhouse?"

I asked her.

She nodded.

"With the dollhouse,"

she said quickly.

"That is what I said."

That night in bed,

I thought about the dollhouse

and the little dolls.

I could not get them

out of my head.

They gave me the creeps.

But I felt like

I <u>had</u> to see them again.

The next day was Saturday.

I went back to Lucy's house.

Before I even knocked,

she opened the door.

It was like she was waiting for me.

"I am getting a new doll today,"

she said to me.

"A kid doll."

Lucy led me up to her room.

I did not see her parents again.

"When will I meet them?" I asked her.

"Today," she said.

Then she started humming.

She seemed really happy.

I peered inside her dollhouse.

Now the dolls were in the kitchen.

There was no doubt about it.

They looked scared!

When Lucy was not looking,

I picked up the mother doll.

She did not feel like my dolls at home.

She felt warm!

I looked closely at her.

She stared up at me.

She looked so real.

Then the doll blinked!

And she jumped out of my hand.

This was no doll.

It was a real live person,

just much, much smaller.

What was going on?

Behind me Lucy started to laugh.

"See?" she said.

"I told you you would meet

my mother and father."

This doll was not a doll.

It was Lucy's mother!

And the father doll was Lucy's father.

What had she done to them?

And what was she going to do to me?

Lucy was staring at me.

Was she some kind of witch?

The two little dolls cried,

"Run away! Run away!"

So I did.

I ran and ran and ran.

But I was barely moving.

And the door was getting bigger.

Or maybe . . .

I was getting smaller.

I ran into the hall.

I <u>was</u> getting smaller!

Up ahead was the front door.

It was open just a crack.

I dove for it.

My knees got scraped.

My headband flew off my head.

But I made it.

Right away,

I felt a tingle in my legs,

in my arms,

in my head.

I was back to my right size again!

I did not wait a second.

I took off—fast—for home.

On Monday, Lucy was not in school.

Later, I walked past her house.

There was a sign out front.

It said "For Sale."

The door was open just a crack.

I could not stop myself from going inside.

The house was empty.

Every last table and chair was gone.

So were the pink curtains,

and so was the dollhouse.

The only thing left

was something small and red

on the floor.

I bent down and picked it up.

It was my headband.